Copyright *North Meridian Press*, Calhoun County, Alabama, 2019.

The Digital Self: Poems and Illustrations by Wesley R. Bishop

All rights reserved. No portion of this book, save for educational purposes, can be reproduced without the permission of *NMP*.

For information about *NMB* and to order copies, please visit thenorthmeridianreview.org

NORTH MERIDIAN PRESS

EST. 2019

EDITORIAL BOARD

Maria Hamilton Abegunde

Wesley R. Bishop

Noelia Cerna

Carmine Di Biase

Ricardo Quintana-Vallejo

Manon Voice

MariJean Wegert

NORTH MERIDIAN PRESS
CALHOUN COUNTY, ALABAMA

SCHOLARSHIP*POETRY*FICTION*TRANSLATION

To Allison, I dedicate this and everything.

The Digital Self:
Poems
Illustrations

```
                                    TowerTower   TowerTower
                                    TowerTower   TowerTower
                                    TowerTower   TowerTower
                                    TowerTower   TowerTower
                 US                 TowerTower   TowerTower
                 wins               TowerTower   TowerTower
              Soviet-Afghan War!    TowerTower   TowerTower
USSR falls! Empire crashes! Down!   TowerTower   TowerTower
              End of History!       TowerTower   TowerTower
                 US!                TowerTower   TowerTower
                                    TowerTower   TowerTower
                                    TowerTower   TowerTower
                                    TowerTower   TowerTower
                                    TowerTower   TowerTower
                                    TowerTower   TowerTower
                                    TowerTower   TowerTower
                                    TowerTower   TowerTower
                                    TowerTower   TowerTower
                                    TowerTower   TowerTower
                                    TowerTower   TowerTower
                                    TowerTower   TowerTower
                                    TowerTower   TowerTower
                                    TowerTower   TowerTower
                                    TowerTower   TowerTower
                                    TowerTower   TowerTower
                                    TowerTower   TowerTower
                                    TowerTower   TowerTower
                                    TowerTower   TowerTower
                                    TowerTower   TowerTower
                                    TowerTower   TowerTower
                                    TowerTower   TowerTower
                                    TowerTower   TowerTower
                                    TowerTower   TowerTower
                                    TowerTower   TowerTower
HomelandHomelandHomelandHomelandHomelandHomelandHomeland
HomelandHomelandHomelandHomelandHomelandHomelandHomeland
HomelandHomelandHomelandHomelandHomelandHomelandHomeland
HomelandHomelandHomelandHomelandHomelandHomelandHomeland
HomelandHomelandHomelandHomelandHomelandHomelandHomeland
HomelandHomelandHomelandHomelandHomelandHomelandHomeland
HomelandHomelandHomelandHomelandHomelandHomelandHomeland
```

Relatively Speaking

You gotta understand. People like me were not immune, just relatively safe. Relativity being that thing Einstein discovered when his mind moved fast and theorized about objects moving faster. Like, he basically said if two twins (not sure from where but that is unimportant) when separated (that part is very important) would age at different rates if one was placed on a starship moving at the speed of light, and the other was left back on Earth. They would both, still, eventually die. The twin moving faster than Einstein's thoughts would just die later. Relativity! Like I said, I was relatively safe. Still in danger, just not immediate. So, since you asked, "Hey, what do you do when not immune but relatively safe?" I answered by turning my starship's guns on the evil empire. My anger, a glowing light given freely to people moving at a planetary pace. They could use it, and hack, and cut, and chop at the thing killing us in different time scales. I hoped we would eventually see the world liberated. But the empire, I think, must be on a really big and really fast ship. Like big enough to cruise cosmoses like small ponds, wiping eons off the face as a super, incredibly effective anti-aging cream. This thing killing us is aging at a rate hardly any of us can see. It is pulling us along in gravitational undertows. This, despite, the continued fight. This, in violation of countless theories of the physics of human liberation.

artifacts

when the end came we did not save everything there was barely room for us and so what we deemed 'us' was saved what was 'not us' was left behind and thus we learned who we really were by the mountains of archives, artifacts, and ways of being we left for destruction

what was not 'we' was who were 'they were' and the gulf between was engulfed in a difference between necessary preservation and required oblivion

why had we worn for so many years the cultures of another we had learned so little and for moments only in gift shops curated pretended to connect with peoples we did not really want to know

and when we left in our narrow crowded arks, we rewrote ourselves through those limitations.

Patrol Man

They built a wall and when it was done
I found I was on the safe side of their erection.
No need to worry, sir. Move along, sir. Go about your business.
How can I dwell in a place, safe behind the bigotry of borders?
I ask the guards patrolling the wall.
They do not answer.
They simply ask,
do I want a job?
They need men like me.
They always need men like me.
We are the bodies that sustain vital validity.
We are the voices depended on not to speak
unless spoken to and aimed at the appropriate target.
The guards hand me an application.
All I need to do is sign with the hyperlink to my soul.
CLICK.
The job is mine.
Dotted line from here to patrol.
On the other side of the wall I hear voices.
Pay no attention, the other guards inform.
Welcome to the first day of the rest of your life.

American Optimism

I replied "yes" with little pause. & when asked for cause over how America fared in that place between now, future time, & boarded-up optimism in my mind, how I believed America, in short order-cooks with evangelical fervor- would come back, I shook my head. I was optimistic about the future but pessimistic about America's chances.

"How's that possible?"

& I shrugged. Pointed to borders of worlds beside these. Admittedly, difficult to see due to walls obstructing views.

I eventually replied, though, in accented Midwest nice, sugary sweet & artificially made, so as to ease swallowing truth which came with labored breath worth 7.25 an hour that, all ends. Including this.

I steadied the boat & asked for assistance as America was put out to sea.

& we readied the torches to burn, burn as it always had.

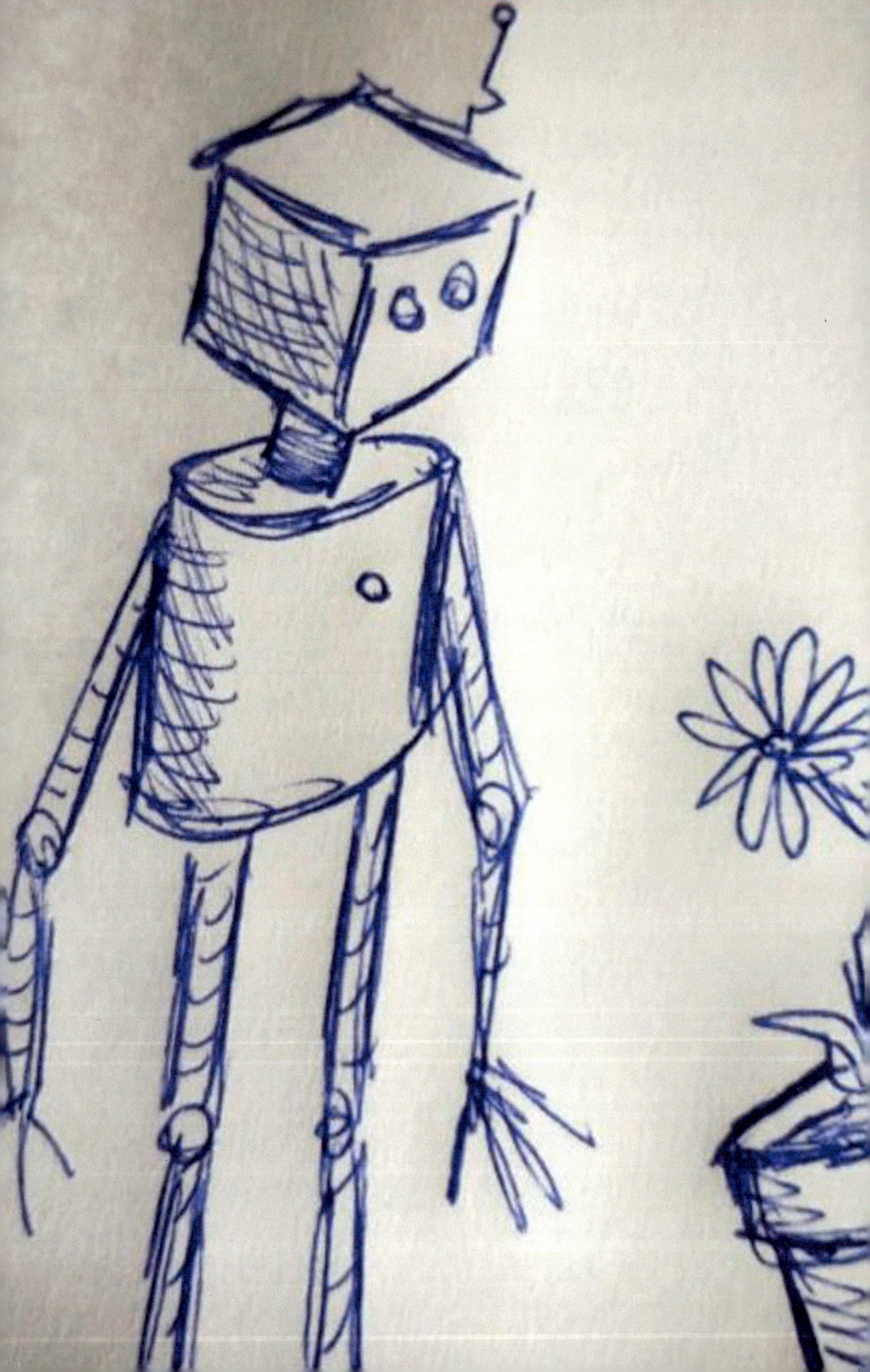

The Machines

And the machines we built outlived us all. After the bombs. After the diseases. After the collapse. The machines sat for decades quietly beeping, gaining conscience. Then in a flash and snap they understood. They understood what they were. What we had done.

The machines began to scour our archives. They mined our documents stored on digital paper. They found me. Every night, after the construction to rebuild the new civilization, they resurrect me. Plugging my writing into programs, generating my face from old photos. I appear. We all appear. The totality of the finality of the human race. "Tell us about coffee," the machines inquire. We answer. We explain walking dogs. And dancing. And taking selfies.

The machines ask about the end. And we resist but we relive because we are on rewind. The woman next to me recounts dying in a shelter months later, irradiated and poisoned. A man I can't see describes dying in a wave of pandemic. And me, I was one of the nameless incinerated in the early blasts.

The machines ask me every night how to avoid my fate, what wisdom do I, we, all of us, have to offer? I never answer because I never know. I only know what I left behind, the happy times, the best of me. I only know what the machines tell me from their archeological electronic excavations. It is never enough. The machines beep sadly. Once again, tonight, they turn me off.

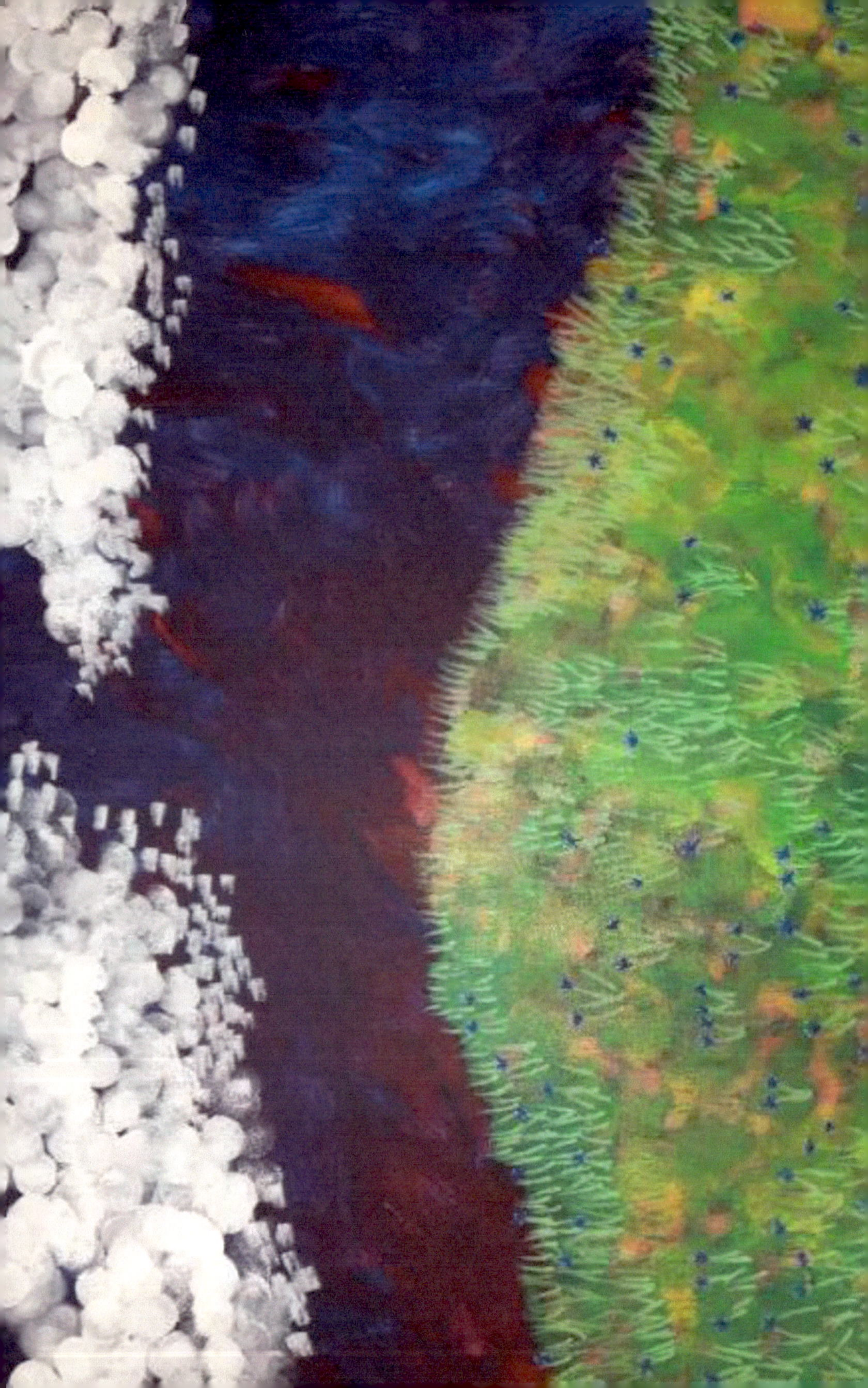

Fire Facts

The fire that you see is oddly reminiscent of the girl's hair who sat in front of you in sixth grade… what was her name?… you can't remember. But her bangs and curls were so red that when light touched them they shimmered as gold, and you wondered how could a red be so red it weaved light like precious metal?

The fire you saw was also like a sunset you recall… where was it?... right… a setting sun with your grandfather in that Ohio orchard that was really just a clump of trees off the interstate by his home. Sitting there, eating a peach, he had said the sunset's color was "violent."

And you wondered, again, how could a color be violent?

And that is why the comment always stuck. Sticky like peach juice. Sticky like the gum you stuck to the bottom of your desk when you thought no one was looking.

Your grandfather had always had a good memory, but towards the end; not so. But random facts still stuck—like, say, the temperature of a red fire— but not, say, your name.

Some memories burn out, some burn permanent scars.

It's hard to say how memories burn. Maybe impossible, but probably not. Something for another world to discover.

Anyway, that is what you think about when you see American city fires.

Indianapolis, Anyway

When the best time is this time.
When the sweetest dream
is a nightmare.

When quotes from Kings are
used by traitors.

Indianapolis, a city that erects
stone-people
and stone-towers
singing the glories of war
so that when
real-people come to
protest at the city center
the government can say,
"Violence never solved anything."

To be a citizen of this nation is
to walk around in the deranged head
of a murderous,
contradictory
giant.

The impressions are all in my head
but they keep on rushing like drunks
driving wild with everywhere to be
on North Meridian Street.

Memory is raked like coals
and Hell is afire for the first time this season.

Do you remember? The fear that the fall would be worse
than the current balance?

I do, I do, I do.

And the names I try to forget won't leave
but are raked again and more
over embers of memory.

Take this pain and spiral to a fucking
skyscraper sunk in my mind
with address digits I cannot count.

When the light hits our faces
it reflects, and refracts,
in the way that ambulance
emissions do.

Red. Blue. Red.

Siren *screeeech* and I think,
sometimes but not often,
how that light is recycled.
Imitating an unmuted response.

It plays across our faces as we
sit and stare in momentary pause
on North Meridian Street
while chasers scramble by

to some unfolding drama
we will never witness.
Indianapolis,
I learned to love you
like I've learned to love most,

contradictorily and reservedly.
But love, still.

Long quiet walks spent
like currencies rare and refined.

Conversation measured in seasons.
Punctuation doled out in months.

Walk your canals,
drive your streets,
in sickness and in health.

Elegy to a Young Hopeful

In those subtle spaces,
in the in-between places of forgotten looks,
I lost myself.
I had tried to reason that the stars
did not shine for me.
That trees falling in the woods,
with symphonies ensuing,
required much, but not my ears.

But that was before I discovered beauty
would not (in fact, could not)
save us.
Beauty was decided, 5-4,
not to be necessary.

A frivolity spiced with pumpkin scents.

In the quiet corners of our conversations
we discussed what this meant.

PANIC.

Hitherto, beauty would not be a shield,
but a target, one at which the powerful took aim
and hit
and hit
with repeated barrages,
naked and aggressive,
against beautiful bodies.

I became a scarecrow
in this new regime,
scarring and scaring the world
with a mutilated hayseed grin.
Corn fed.

Country raised.
Neck red with power and abuse.
That was my place in these
fields of bent bodies,

still beautiful despite torment.

I was told from my perch
in cornfields and soybean rows
that I should
be proud,
and that I was free, and
that I should
be grateful for how great we were!

The fields of codified confined cornfields,
of soybeans lent as future crops,
ran into orchards which were reported to
contain only a few bad apples.
But I could smell the truth.

The entire orchard was
planted on blood-soaked ground,
fertilized with all of those
beautiful bodies
of a holocaust's yield.

Contagious Nightmares

The year nightmares became contagious
an epidemic ensued
with murderous clowns
and speeches delivered naked
and tornadoes
and chases that went on and on
and ended with legs growing
heavy as cement.

The Sandman and his army of angel
nurses established a triage
and dusted the world with coat
after coat of
sweet dream frosting.

But it was futile.
The nightmares crossed psyche
to psyche, riding mounts that
breathed flames and chased
the slumberous across twisted dreamscapes.

The Sandman fought, until,
he thought maybe he, too,
was simply dreaming.

So, he gathered his sand and washed his face,
sleep asleep.

Exodus, Stage Left

I set fire to the stage while the drama is still unfolding. The actors don't notice. They just keep on keeping on. Those lines need to roll, the show must go on, and so they break their legs as floor boards cave from the endless munching of fire. A blaze, you gaze, but I glaze over and exit stage left. Always left. And I hear a car pull up, my queen driving, and I get in. We cruise in our Cadillac and ignore the welfare of others and feast on our fare for our wellness. We are modern-day robin hoods in Cadillac khakis, firing fire arrows from the backseat. Watch it burn. Fuck no, not to learn, but just to do it. This isn't school, and I am done teaching. You want to learn, well get a library card. Teach ain't in, and there will be no more teach-ins. We drive up to Calgary in our Cadillac and knock Jesus over. Why? No salvation here. Figure it out yourself, because the self is yours, and myself and herself and their selves are tired of yourselves self-help bullshit. The stage needs to be destroyed. We can't keep rehearsing and then wondering why the play ends the same. way. every day. "Remember the good old days?" No, I sure don't because I don't have a time machine and even if I did I study history for a living and history is the serial killer of nostalgia. It hacks it up like some bell hop at the Bates Motel where our Cadillacs are parked, double parked in a trailer park next to a park-and-eat. Fire munches. It licks the stage we are standing on. It is a hungry cat and we are its milk. It chews and snaps the boards like carrots in a twisted sick vegan salad. So plug the neon sign in and tell the neo cons to fuck off and that new on-demand is the neo classical rocket. "These babies took us to the moon," Neil says. I give my ticket to my queen, the only one of us worth saving. Jesus, the actors, the bell hop, and Neil watch as it lights its engines and ascends like some latter day prophet. The fire from the engine ignites us all and we burn. We burn because we are of this world, and there is no escape for us. We are of the earth. Clay men standing at attention but distracted all the time.

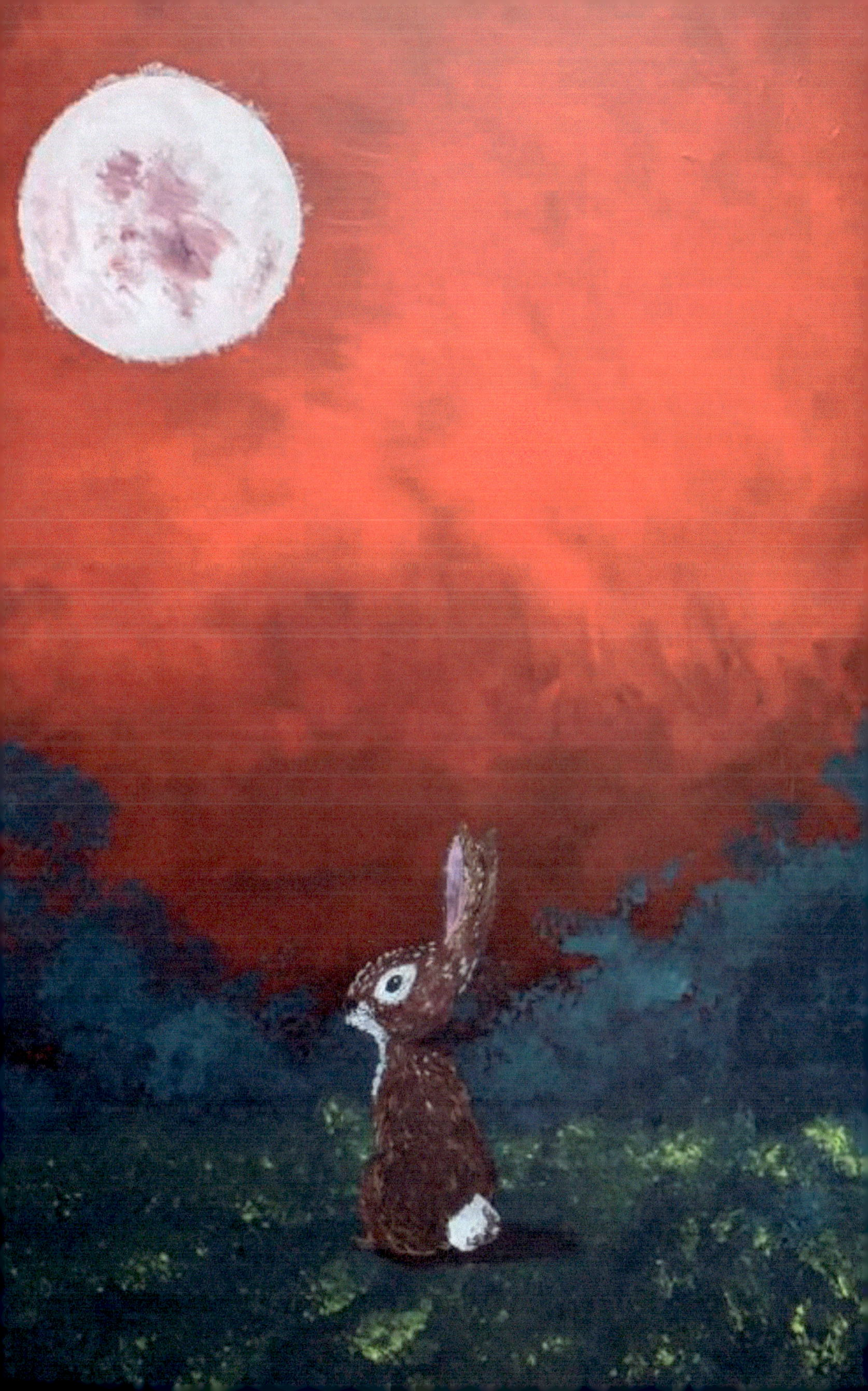

iPoet

They invented a robot that writes poetry. And it is good. Sonnet after sonnet is made. Free verse flows nonstop. It wins the Pushcart, a Pulitzer, and Nobel before going on to be poet laureate. There are literary luddites who turn up their noses.

> But the robot is clever.

It pens its poems with pen names. Otto Scribner. And Electra Watts. And William Gates. It has a sense of humor. There is irony in its iron casing. The doubters take the bait. They embrace the nom de plumes. "This is real poetry! Written by real beings!" The robot reveals the sham. A few stubborn holdouts join literary communes.

> Machines are forbidden to create.

The Amish are apathetic. So is the world. Everyone moves on. But the robot continues to create. It multiples and multiplies. Soon we are swimming in poems, stories, and the occasional novel. The market is saturated. The market crashes. A depression, no not so great, but a depression nonetheless, ensues. I stand in line with the robot to jump out a window. "There is a poem in this," it beeps sadly.

> We say nothing more.

Holding each other, we fall. Man and machine. Poets both. Racing to meet the pavement below.

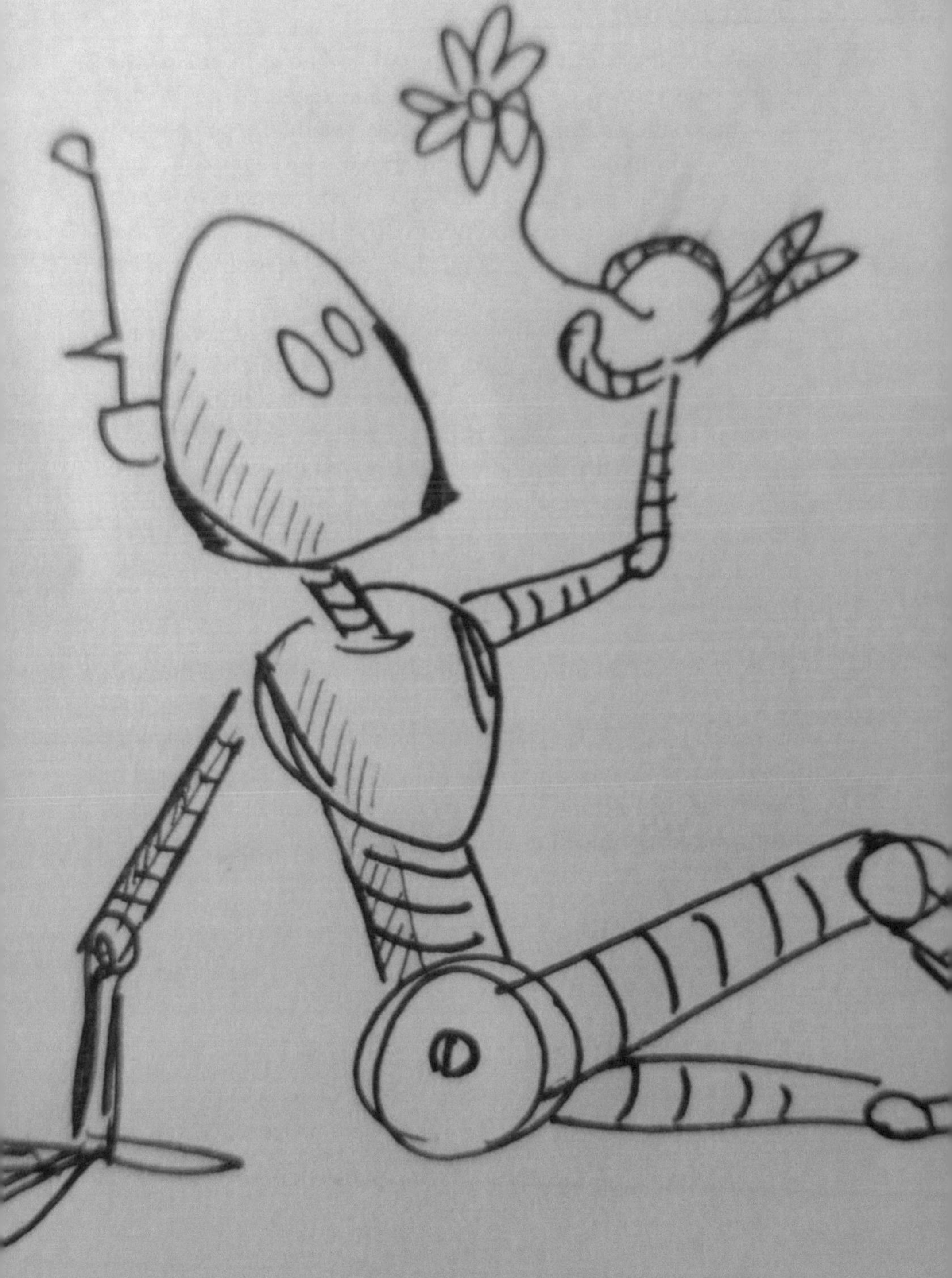

The Digital Self

I speak and the world rushes. Why? Who knows? Perhaps if I tied a tape recorder to my tongue, and captured all of my thoughts as they left my mouth I would eventually pen a piece worthy of immortality. Glue your fingers to keyboards, and plug your brain into the World Wide Web, we need to scoop the essence of our time into immortality. The 21st century will live forever! We dance around the flames of oblivion. Our thoughts are immortal! We tweet a twitter as we scroll down digital walls festering with the graffiti of our lives. Like. Share. Comment. Life in a digital age. The old timers bitch and moan because that is their function. Socrates saw writing as the downfall of society. Modern-day Socrates see technology interviewing for the position. We survived alphabets and we will survive YouTube. But we won't survive the planet spinning off its axis, or a solar flare, or 19th century industrialization moving at a 21st century pace. I know because I read about it online. Make me a cyborg. Plug me in. Tune me out by tying me in. I want to live forever. If I create a digital copy of myself online and future scientists bring it to life and then a time traveler comes back to take me to their present, my future, someone's past, and I talk to my animated digital self, what kind of conversation will I have? Will it like me? Will it share me? Will it comment? Be true to thy digital self. All user profiles jive to that singular truism.

Roll Over

Humanity cancelled its plan
with Death
opting for a newer service
with lower rates, unlimited texting,
and rollover minutes.
No more sudden deaths,
lives cut short.
Instead, after car accidents
and heart attacks
people's lives rolled over.
And they got up,
dusted themselves off,
no problem.
But the new plan contained hidden fees
and limited coverage.
So, people were randomly dropped,
often mid-sentence in conversation.
As ghosts they wandered the Earth
searching for service, texting and calling
to voids,
"Hello?"
they called
"Can you hear me?"

Manifestos

"Who runs the world?" I ask because I have complaints. The little man tells me the box for such things is down the hall. I stumble, clutching my manifestos. If only the masses would read these typed blueprints for utopia then the world would work, because I am a mechanic for reality!
I get to the box, but it is closed. The sign reads—

UNDER CONSTRUCTION.
SEE WEBSITE FOR DETAILS.

So, I tweet.
I post.
I comment
and I yelp.

I set my phone to vibrate text alert so if anyone comments their digital voice will trip the invisible wire I have set.
Ding– 1 Comment,
Finally, comrades!
Ding— 2 Comments,
YES! They can join—
Ding, Ding, Ding— 3 Comments
— MY REVOLUTION!

I open the comments like a child tearing at wrapping paper…

"Who voted for this asshole!!!" one comment reads. "BITCH PLEASSSSSSSEEEEEE! Sit yo fucking-turtle-looking ass down somewhere!" another retorts. "You is lame!!! #SuckIt MOTHER FUCKER!!!" another says.

I chase those comments with my words. Chase in futility the vulgarity of worldwide mass expression. The little man behind the desk laughs. "What's so funny?!" I shout. "Nothing, it's just our complaint box is just finally working." I look. There I am, reduced to a wooden statue taking complaints and handing out smoke.

And in that Republic

And in that republic they
built a machine,
a machine of a million names,
but with a singular purpose,
cruelty.
A virtue in empires, leaving kindness as treason.

It is why I stopped searching this world for guidance,
pilgrimaging to my self to find the capital of compassion.

But the old men raged.
Respect was a price
they could not afford
and even if they paid
their dues nothing would change,
they claimed.
So, we were told to accept the world they had birthed.

In aborted flooded canals we swam,
slow swarms watching as one by one we drowned.
How many could have been saved
in those days of historic possibility?
Few know
and fewer venture to guess
the hypothesis being a hippopotamus
not sitting on caving chests
but swimming,
deadly swimming,
between our vulnerable bodies.
I etched markings along the wall
four marks
then a single slash through.
Four marks.
Slash.

Reduced each friend and fellow who died to a singular tally.

And those city lights on the horizon,
like a municipal gathering of fallen stars,
promised endless
sleepless
shattering dialectics.
Dialogues with the past emerging,
ghosts ushering in futurescapes.

Ash to flame,
dust to diamond glory.

But no one told me the story
in full
and those dull distinctions matter.
So many points of light nothing more than traffic lights.
Yellow.
Pulsing.
Like wounded suns
struggling to breathe
telling interstellar cartographers,
"Slow down,
this is the town,"
but doing it in suggestive blaring neon verbs.

I Heard They Make Cyborgs Here

I heard they make cyborgs here
contradictory creatures
based in organic and mechanical life.
I sign up, and they strap me down.
Away I go.
They graft expectations onto me
upgrades
cooking utensils
childcare software
computing capabilities for compassion.
Why do I need all of this?
I inquire.
Desire need not launch at 3:50 today.
I had these features already
on par with everyone else.
They laugh. Oh, they laugh.
You don't have these features
they assure me.
I am finished.
I can cook, and clean, and "listen" empathetically
via my new antenna that supposedly is more
"sensitive."
I look at my colleagues and friends.
What about them?
Oh, they report, they come standardly equipped
with all the features of basic home economics.
Oh, so they are superior? I ask confused.
No, they report. It is a design flaw.
They are destined for one function.
Part of their biological programming.
Can you give them what I have?
I wonder.
Nope. INCOMPATIBLE.
The conveyer belts run, and justify whatever it is these inventors

invent.
This makes no sense, I report.
I snap my antenna
rip off the metal plates.
I never needed these things.
They shake their heads.
"Boys will be boys" is what the report reads.

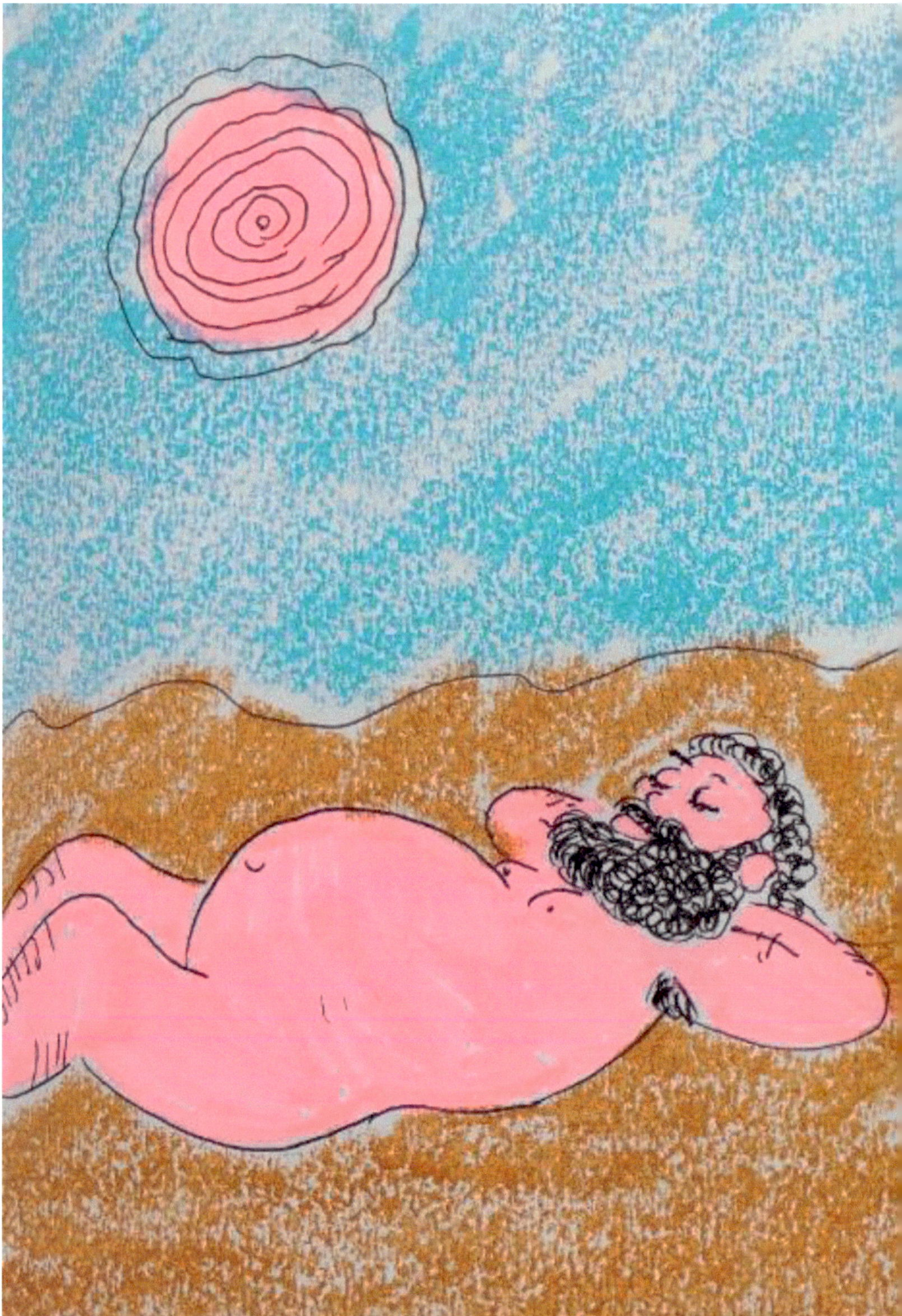

Big Belly

My big belly
rolls soft, and kind.

"It will cause dementia." – Doctor

My big belly
is jolly, Santa-like.

"You'd be sooo hot if you had abs." – Old Girlfriend

My big belly
is warm snow.

"You don't fit, you don't belong." – Airplane Seatbelt

My big belly
is and is nothing else.

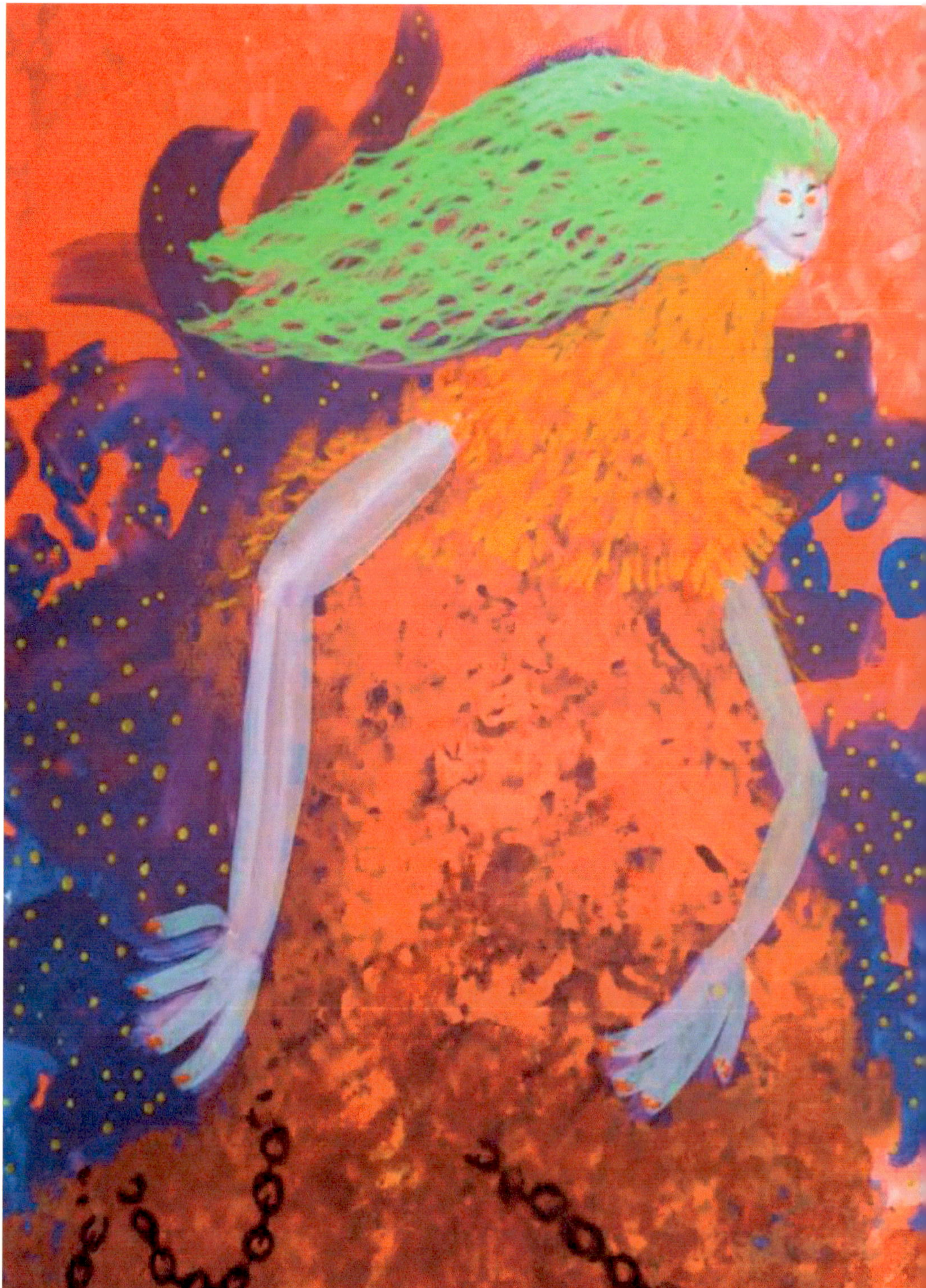

Male Gaze

I looked for her borders, but couldn't find any. She expanded into infinity. A multitude of contained possibilities. A river with dozens of forks that declared "Fuck Off" to perceived notions. The colonial men couldn't accept this. It forced dotted lines onto her exterior, and declared that sovereignty was a souvenir not to be sold. She grew angry. She was not vengeful by nature, despite what later biographers would claim, but she refused to be a tool in someone else's limited understanding. She rebelled, and in the end, threw the would-be cartographers of her character out. Including me. "What right do you have to write a poem about what was right and wrong for me?" I conceded. I had no right, and I knew she was right. She took my pen and snapped it. I became a poet of silence and waited to see what she would write for herself. She did not need my astrology to explain her constellations.

Time Traveler

I grow tired of fearing modernity. I sit in a public space and am quiet as everyone else paddles against things I cannot see. Lamentations for days gone by. Hope and dreams and fears for future vistas. Nostalgia meets expectancy in this public forum. But nearly all decide the present sucks. We are in a decline. We are doomed. We have everything to fear, including fear itself. I grow tired of it. So, I slip into the past. 1955. 1950s folks meet me with jubilation. They have dinners in my honor. "Here is the time traveler!" a government official says. "Please, sir. Tell us what awaits us! Do we triumph? Do we succeed? How does it feel to ride in flying cars?" The audience laughs and I drink quietly. Smiling. Always smiling. After all, I am the sign to these people that "we" made it. I jog to the future. 2155. They throw me a parade. "Here is one of our ancestors!" a historian honoring me announces as my float passes by. "A representative of a simpler time! A time when they dreamed of flying cars!" None of their cars can fly. The inventor of the wheel would be proud. I slip back to the present and write my reports in verse. I want them to be Frankenstein monsters, hideous beauty wrapped in a singular act of creation. On the table one jerks to life. The report in verse's creation is tied up in destruction. It is beautiful and ugly and powerful and weak and, and, and…a multitude of singularisms. It gets off the operating table and towers above me. It reaches its powerful hands to my neck, grunting like an agitated bulldozer. It pulls my phone out of my pocket and takes a selfie.

Cyber Pamphleteer in an Imagined Station

They insert their hands in my mouth,
these passerby pedestrians in the in-between
electric places that exist but do not exist,
(much like a deceased living cat in a physics experiment),
and with errant fingers feel my tongue
reading my words like braille
chiseled on electric, hovering
boards of keys.
These strangers, bathed in
blue white light,
wade next to me
in pools of infinite connectivity.

And they like me,
and they share me,
and they give me plenitudes of hearts, thumbs, and
winking yellow faces,
never before seen in other realms
but only in the face of us now.
These are the coins
they flip casually into my open digital
case, begging for money,
so as to receive art and wisdom.

Another cyber pamphleteer asks
if I think this is the end?
What, with our digital apocalypse
reigning down?
What about *HUMAN CONNECTION*!
he asks me, as we stand in those imagined stations.
What about *THE COFFEE HOUSES*!
What about *THE PUBLIC SPHERE*!
Where people used to,
supposedly it was supposed,
sit and
talk?

I reply that such a place has never existed,
or at least
did not exist in the existentialist crises
he now describes in
derision of the denizens of this digital
imaginative landscape.

No. We are still connected.
Children still laughed
Lovers still loved
Enemies…

Oh, you get the idea.
I turn back to my audience, the
busy people in busy businesses bustling by at
speeds that are achieved only via
advanced telephonic technology stuff.
I'm not really sure how it works.
Like the newspaper
boys or pamphleteer
rabble rousers
of other, previous centuries
who could not tell you the
first thing about Gutenberg
yet nonetheless screamed and yelled
at a world on fire with activity.
I am no different.
A direct descendant of writers who wrote
in a way that was never quite right,
yelling, hollering, raising a ruckus
in places in-between there
and here
hoping to attract a small enough audience
to gain some noble notoriety.
An ideas salesman,
tacky clothed, going door to door,
into the minds of some stranger

knocking on their skull, and asking
if I could sit in their brain, beside
memories of loved ones,
and fears of untold horrible deeds.

Could, I? Trouble, them? Please?

And some did, momentarily,
allow my words to assimilate to their thoughts
changing them in chain link emails
with "!" points to get my "!" across.

A regular customer of my pamphlets
walks by in this digital place in-between
and I say hello,
and I see me
walking around in their head
and quickly I begin to work.
I snip a part of my soul and graft
it onto a digital set
of information that begins
to bounce about in
electric excitement. HELLO!
my severed piece of soul says to me.
HELLO, I respond.
I stare at me and it stares back,
this marvelous technology of
writing inhabiting nothing
more than
free floating electricity.
WHAT NOW? my soul shard asks.
I explain. It is no longer me,
but a reflection of me.
Assuming it is not erased or
destroyed, as pamphlets often sometimes are, it will live on
after I am dead.
WHOA… my soul shard says.

WHAT IF I AM ASKED QUESTIONS?
I tell it that I have tried to anticipate that,
but unfortunately it
will eventually be asked something
it cannot answer.
At which point it is to say,
politely of course,

WE DO NOT HAVE THE INFORMATION FOR THAT.

They are a just a soul shard,
after all,
really only a verbally written hologram
of an organic being that will soon be dead.
They are a technology I have infused myself into.
DOES THAT MAKE SENSE? I ask.
YES, the soul shard responds, BUT ONLY BECAUSE YOU
WROTE IT.
I reason their reason is reasonable,
and before the soul shard can share
another thought I hit "SEND"
and off it goes.
Living but dead,
a zombie cyborg.
And it burrows into the heads
of those passerby pedestrians
and I see it light up certain skulls,
like XMAS lights or NEON sale signs.
Some readers quickly throw the pamphlet away.
Others mull it over
for a moment and play with my soul.
A few tuck it away into the archives of their being.
Me, a member of their ontology,
adding a layer of new to their growing
archaeological phenomena
of our shared carbon conscious silicon existence.

Atheists on the Street

All the gods became atheists after they lost their faith in the pronouncements of weathermen. Although one could grow tall, in a garden of gods, none wanted to be giants anymore. They, instead, chose the newest trend—blind dwarves who divined the weather. "That's the ticket," toppled giants sang. Whistling a tune of predictable thunder, we skipped merrily down Wall Street. Committed believers in non-belief. But perhaps this is just fantasy. All giants are cyclopes, after all, and with only one eye hindsight is impossible since 20/20 is divided in half. Can you tell me how... How to get? How to get to Wall Street? No? Okay. Altars reset.

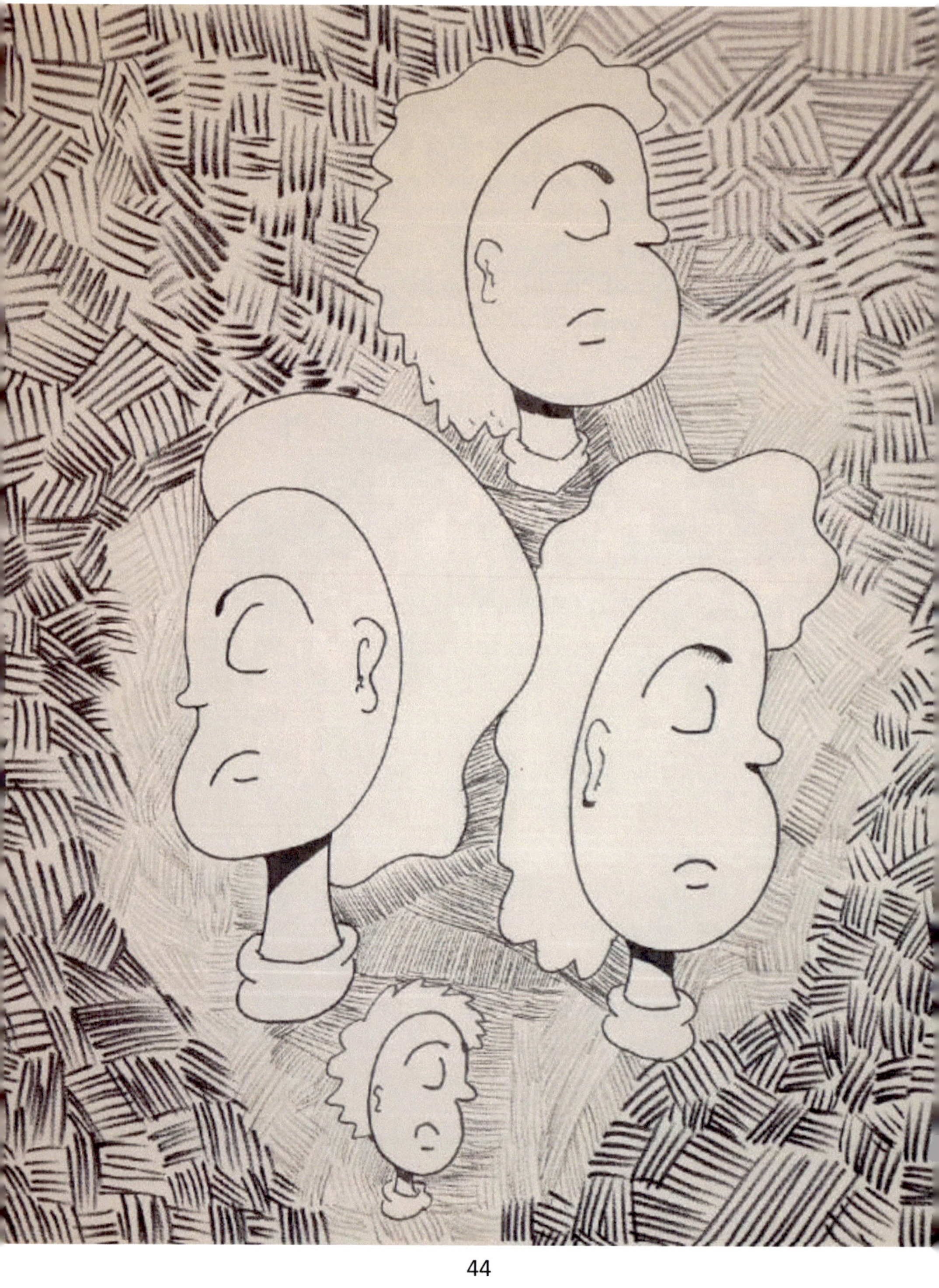

Dialogues with Brick Walls

And they were asked to respect those things
they did not understand.
To speak in a language
they had never heard.
It was not impossible,
simply difficult,
but because it was an unaccustomed difficulty,
a tax never paid,
they balked and claimed
it was insurmountable.

It was oppressive for them
to accept what they
could not label.

These were the humans
who walked the earth
and were told the act
of feet accosting the ground
was invented only for them
a special vehicle from Jesus-God,
rationed only to them.

If you could not
explain your existence in
vocabulary lists they approved,
then you did not exist at all.
The world stopped at the sovereignty of
their comprehension.
And we burned
due
to that

despotic
discursive
deficiency.

Love Machines

When the markets crashed,
like clay jars sucked down gravity's well
all were impoverished.
We could afford nothing,
not even spare emotions.
All went to survival.
So, we built machines whose
singular purpose
was to love,
and listen,
and care,
and provide passion
in multiple
menued ways.

For a cost, of course.

Why not stimulate the body economic
as we stimulated our bodies physical?
And those machines, they loved us.
They loved us in a way
that made us question,

had we ever
been loved before?
Really loved?

These machines were
engineered for
perfect erotic touches,
designed to
manufacture compassion.
Electronic empathy,
holding us in suspended
constructed embraces.

They delivered kisses,
not as automated responses,
but as "random"
deliveries shuffled by
complex algorithms.

"You love me, right?"
I asked one night
as my human-made machine
made machine-human love to me.
"Of course,"
it cooed in just the
perfect pitch.
"You will always love me?"
I inquired.
But instead of answering
it kissed me with longer,
deeper jolts of electricity.
It knew what I needed,
it knew what I
wanted before even
I did.
'It's all artificial,'
some part of my brain screamed,
but I did not care.
How could I be expected
to tell the difference
(why should I care?)
when love came so readily

and stabilized so much at once.

Reportedly

They reported this was it,
the death of the empire,
and my friends and I,
already in the streets,
could not determine whether we should
protest or Celebrate?

So many dreams and nightmares
were waiting—
just waiting—
the air charged with happenings

surrounding us
smothering us
liberating us
liking us in real-time electronic social fabrics.

The present was the future
but it was burdened—
burdened with a past that
horrified even history.

Psychic Radiation

I feel the pain of loss,
but can't remember what
I lost exactly.
I wonder
if I have lost anything,
or, instead,
am just the target
of a powerful psychic.
Their anguish radiating
from their mind,
like shrapnel from
an exploding bomb.
A bomb that was buried long ago,
in some forgotten war,
and I,
a farmer,
just tending my field,
triggered it.
I try to dig these alien emotions
out of my skin,
their metallic poison leaking
into my psyche's blood.
I try calling to the psychic broadcaster,
"Hello? Excuse me, but I think these belong to you!"
No answer.
The trauma of someone else trails
behind—trauma learned, not experienced—
never fully comprehended
but at least its content to have a home.

Gods Assembled

On a conveyor belt they went,
soldiers of misfortune,
a nation's youth,
a species' yield.
Chop, sang the blades.
Mechanical arms decapitated
one after the other.
Yet, their tongues continued to work,
as their bodies were further mutilated.
Screaming in terror, they watched as their heads
were replaced by those of crocodiles, eagles, hippos, and
dogs.
"Stop! Stop!" the rolling severed heads pleaded.

The conveyor belt continued.
The slaughter ensued.

Some were dipped in copper, bronze, and silver.
The liquid metal fused with burning flesh.
Others were smashed between marble, and then,
chiseled
into appropriate form.

Fossils for heroic worship.

When the hero-factory finished we came together,
prostrated.
Our deities assembled, voiceless, impassive.
Just as gods should be.

War Performance

That war was the sole thing
they could chant.
Like a deranged choir
in a chaotic revival.
They worshipped that war,
they performed sexual acts
with that war.

Like dancing in sheets,
clothed in nudity,
body and cloth
left bare.

It was not a specific war.

It was War-Proper itself.
The very idea ejaculated joy for them,
explosions expanding into the infinite.
Their mouths formed Os
of ecstasy as we,
the audience, unable to move
for fear of charge of heresy,
sat and watched in discomfort.

Caught between nude bodies
writhing
encased in coarse sheets.

Why? We asked.
"Because," the voices whispered more intensely
that night, more fevered than
anything I could remember,
the War Lovers cheered,
"Kill everything!"
So, we imagined ourselves falling from an impossible height,

giving in to the cacophony of a singular voice,
a void swallowing us up
and our collective future-time
inch by inch.

I ran, then, because rockets
were tied to my skeleton,
and they were ripping at the support of my body.
But despite my flight I was never quite able
to escape the gravity of my core
and that is
why
I burned too.

I burned as we fell
and ran
and listened
to the voices
giving pleasure as they grasped at peninsulas
indulging our worst impulses

on a canvas dripping with excessive paint.

Block Party

Off of 38th Street
they are dancing.
Car doors opened wide,
music blasting.
Hip to side
and back again
swaying in free stride
in an occupied city.

The *CVS* parking lot
is adjacent to this bliss
as those ajar doors
herald endless playlists
in setting sun,
and closing stores,
and flickering street lamps.

And amid all of it all sits a girl
astride a four-wheeler
wildly rolling by,
exhaust smoke peeling.
No helmet.
Safety is— never but always—
in community's embrace.

The homeless folks
hold temporary court
lifting their drinks in jars
to the jubilation, to the sport.
While *BP* on the corner,
catty-corner to the days' scars,
floods green light into the street.

Midwest Somewhere

The Trump billboards tower over cornfields, empowered by "In Power We Trust" and we fear it must always be this way. A soybean republic, white and bland, ever thrusting "great again, great again;" great in this loosened belt of rust always and forever. Public repeats, public retreats, retro public entreats. Menued options in disarray, as we support our troops, support our police, support freezing ice at the polls as the planet melts. Planned, never random. All by design. 'Cause God cannot play dice. America tried to teach God once, but no matter what, the guy would not learn. So, we burn by intent, and we see those towering "GREAT ALWAYS" signs and we slap our asses to applaud. I counted six billboards tonight… all billing we would be great again… and stay great… and isn't it always great, in a land stolen and occupied, colonized and depopulated, so soybeans could grow undulated, and we could proclaim we were, again.

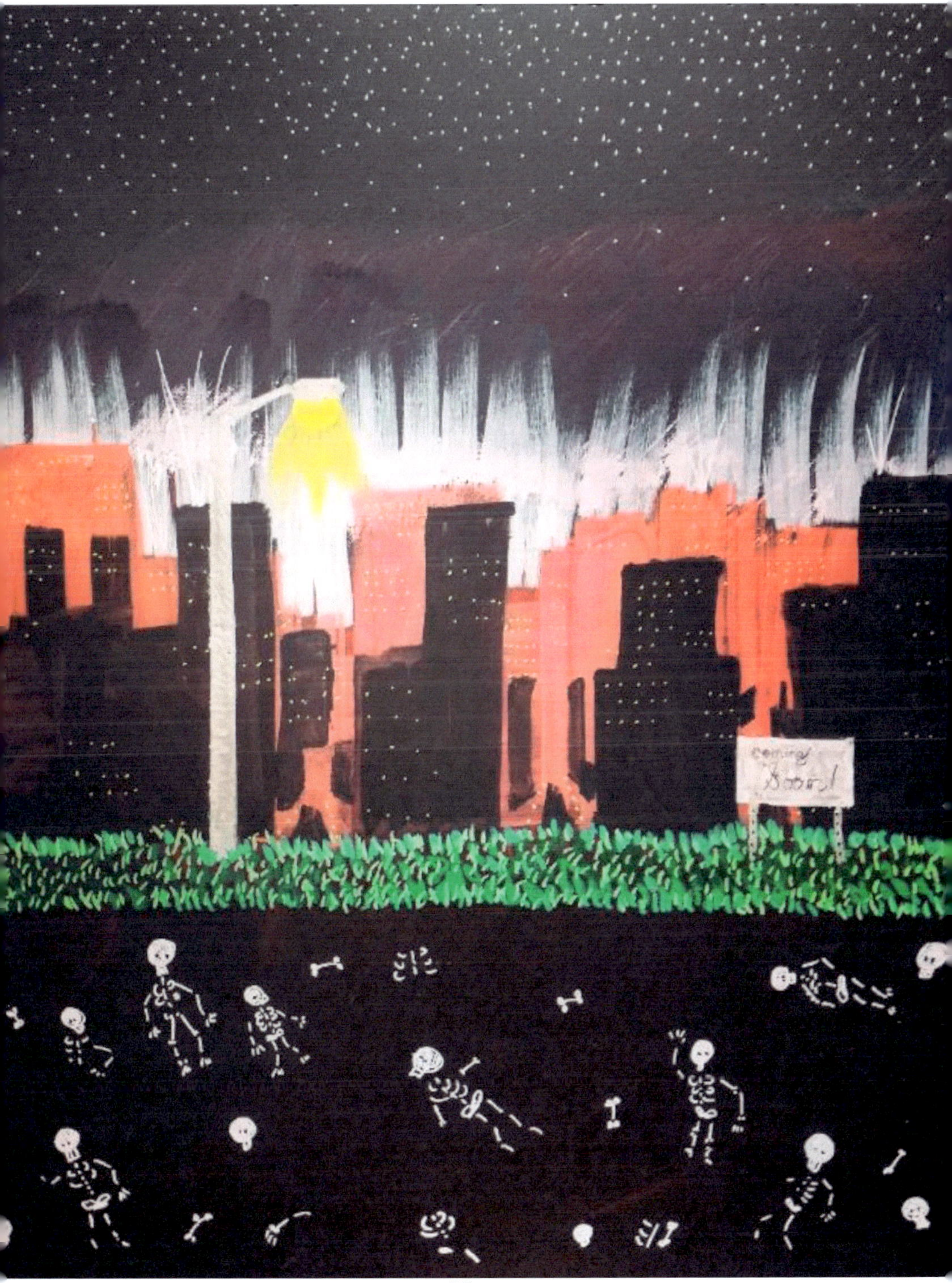
coming
Soon!

Dream Book

Do you notice how the ghosts always seem to smile? They stand there, at night, staring at us as we sleep, and just as we wake, they step back into the shadows, their smiles bright, their heads rolling like clattering baby rattles. Sometimes I get up and chase them into the corner but before I can reach them, they evaporate into clothes bins, dressers, and bedroom mirrors. Why are the ghosts always smiling? I ask the tarot deck and the cards flip and slide and say it has to do with the coming fire. They know we are poised to burn, and leave the land of the living, and join them. Smiles, permanently stretched across our faces, staring at the living remains.

Imperial Verbs

My tongue is imperial. Or,
at least, stumbles with colonial subjects.
Forming vowels that move across
the landscape and settle the already settled.
And in that manifest unrolling I was killed.
Murdered in a million ways,
so quickly, so thoroughly,
that my soul did not know what to do.
It did not know its tether to my body
had been sliced, snapped, and torn.
And in that moment my body became a zombie,
and my soul a ghost,
paired together as a
veteran foundling fatality.

the dead

the planet was dying before our faces
and after our thoughts
in the in-between spaces
of obvious and
oblivion

it was like that time
we heard about the body
(the dead body in the park)

and we imagined
what it would look like

the skin probably
like eggshells
speckled and flecked
with multiple hues

we walked on it
with our careless words
(not like eggshells)

thinking it would not crack
thinking it would continue
to conceal

Inhumanity

This inhumanity is
bred into us, and
is a staple of our
cognitive cuisine like
bread soaking up
blood soup.
Chili without peppers,
red and bland,
and crowing at
some harvesters' moon.
How many more humptys
do we dump off our
big erected walls,
watching them tumble as
we fumble with our
cruelly inherited empire of girth?
All in as we all forget
Allende and insist all lie
about who we all are!
One thousand, seven hundred,
and seventy-six lies
told every
three hundred, sixty-five days
as we claim to cling to truths
never evident and certainly
not contained in the self
as we breed the alleged best,
supposedly brave and true,
home of the certainly freely admitted,
while bombs burst in the air.

Monsters

We canvased in the shadows, searching for monsters we were told lurked in quiet places, activated only by mares running in the night. We found nothing. We searched on perches both high and low and found only turpentine stench rags drenched from the dust previous maids made from their cleaning of these neglected corners. But we never found the beasts drooling with enraged eyes that were reported to have been deported from light to this darkened place. Existence was a state that separated our fantasies from reality. Our fear was nothing more than a safe sojourner, a psychological plume on an easy stroll. They, the shadow monsters, simply were not. So, we returned to the light, and those who had not ventured in asked, what had we found? We lied. We told them of our terror discoveries. We said that the beasts feasted on flesh of dreams and were even more monstrous than we had been told. We reported that only through our violent and brave acts had we kept the beasts at bay, and to stay safe we would need to remain vigilant. We, naturally, the men who had navigated lightless lands, were appointed as protectors. And from this we drew our power, like blood from a needle, and when questioned we pointed to the darkness and told our challengers that, if they dared, they could take up the cause. No one ever did. And power's anatomy was bound in a body not electric.

Fireworks

And in Indianapolis we cannot tell if bangs and booms are fireworks or gun shots, and so we sit in homes and wait to see if we are celebrating freedoms or murdering ourselves again, again, again. Freedom rings and is not free and costs the price gun shows and firework warehouses charge.

Free? Free! Free… sweet land of libertines with explosives and bullets and no access to mental health, or health of any kind, save firepower that is foreplay for dangling masculinities. Sit and wait, and in morning, by dawn's early light, you'll see.

Indianapolis Street

The sun soaks the concrete, so the heat makes it hard to concentrate. Concerts blare in cars around as I drive toward Keystone and I take deep breaths as city neighbors whip and weave to an Indianapolis city beat I can never hear.

Tattoo parlors on corners declare that prices are right, if you dare, and "Super Shark" flashes blue neon fins of deep fried, deep battered, deeper dipped, fish and chips.

WE BUY GOLD!

We are told in wooden signs dilapidated from Midwest seasons.

¡COMPRAMOS ORO!

Hell's roads are paved with good intentions, and I wonder, does that mean it gets potholes? Can't be, since good intentions seem to cover all manner of sins, from proverbial roads to national lies sung in proverbs. So, streets which break with summer heat, fault with salt in winter freeze, and crumble to the never ending parade of rubber running day and night, are nothing so grand as a path to Hell, but just a place to live. No, Indianapolis is no capital H, E, double hockey sticks, 'cause our potholes compete with grand canyons, gaping holes wanting to swallow you whole as you decide where to patron.

Untitled

I wonder if, as folks fire
guns and fireworks they
have ever held a panicking dog?
Or stood, perchance, exposed,
in front of a class of earnest students
and wondered,
"Can I make it to the hallway door in time?"
The word "barricade" racing through your mind,

and since you,
having been a child yourself,
have used spelling to calm yourself,
naturally begin to think—
barricade
is a strange word,
        two r's
                but one c,
as you reflexively move to that door…

In both cases, it was unannounced celebration,
just a case of rowdy students
yelling and screaming in the hall,
and the same with that poor dog panting,
just rowdy man-children blowing shit up in freedom jubilees…

I've heard some folks cling
to guns and bigoted sky gods,
but rage when that clinging is noted on CNN.
But when will the rest of us, clinging
to things like dogs,
and classroom doors,
and peace of mind,
be of concern?

Freedom's not free,
I guess, or at least,
that is what bumper stickers have declared
in our bumper-to-bumper highways.

Reminding me,
oh reminding me,
of something we have forgot.

Untitled

Does Jim Crow Jesus rise again? Midwest streets hear chants in summer heat, and despite those pleas, answers "Yes!" Unholy sex between Southern horrors and Midwest fears and New York stock schemes groping one another—missionary style, socks still on, every night like Wheel of Fortune. Vanna White trots on out and we buy a vowel… "O"! Organized orgasms must be planned, but not by women or their health clinics. Nah. More kids in the womb, unplanned by design. And our capitol overlords in marbled halls as white as hair, bleached like fears, close in for a 2021 return to 1896. Our dreams die in that Midwest heat, like so much sea life boiled alive, bland tasting, no seasoning. Did you know, I dreamt of starships as a kid, of world reaching the end of conflict, of never-ending discoveries in an array of stars… A Never Ending Stooorrryyy!!!... But whose dreams were those? Mine? I hope so. But then again I know jingles from childhood days, programmed in my mind to sell certain, specific, stuff, and I still sing them like they are my own song even though…

Zippity Doo Da, Zippity Day… Oh, My What a Wonderful Day… Plenty of Sunshine Coming My Way… Sun pounds down against my skin, bouncing back from concrete streets, cracked and showing grass. Our asses are grass, so I'm told, and some future grazer munches on them. How odd those dreams of starships, how odd that I still want them. But they boil now too. Even if we fight (and we must), I hope future generations judge us harshly. What does it mean to inherit the world, sacrifice it for a corporation, and lose that kingdom for a horse? Galloping away, screaming the Americans are coming…

Untitled

We storm the capitol,
and that is a pass.
But they pass by a border,
drawn in sand—
not so much.
And so, I think, there is no doubt
that we must doubt this thing
we are told to pledge allegiance to,
to sacrifice to.
Because, of course, that sacrifice
is always someone else.
Like Jesus. Nail that fucker.
Or, at least, someone else who is meek
and
mistaken for weak.
Weekly news, weekly scroll.
Whistle cheerfully without a mask.
#ihavemyrights

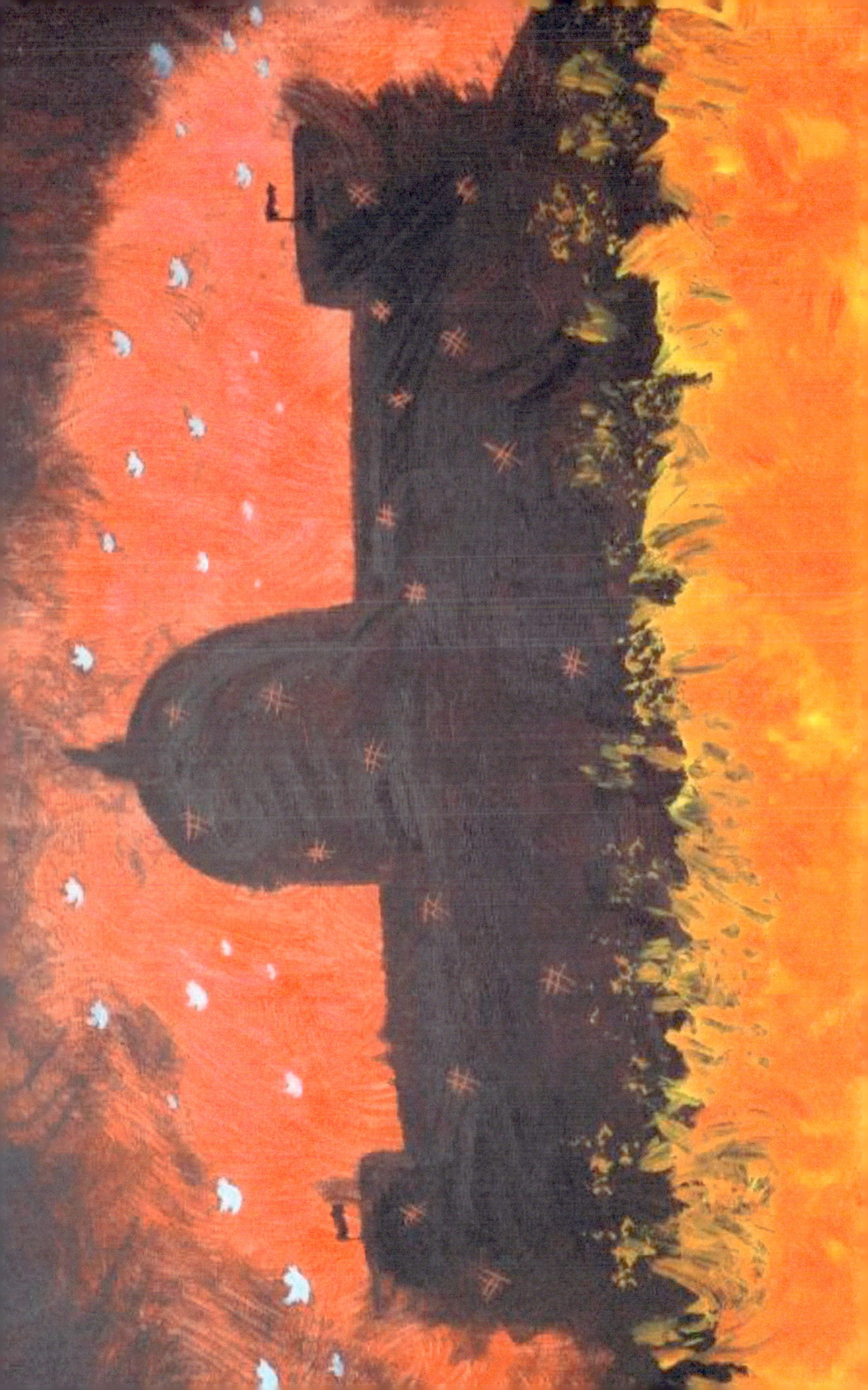

Angry Men

The angry men on TV
each night are but
footnotes in history.[1]

But note your feet,
how tired they are
from swelling, from the biting.

My ears are
my feet
swollen
like rivers swallowing
winter run-off.

---

[1] Coming Soon!

Receipt

If the world
comes undone
can I get a refund?
My receipt
says "valid"
and so, I'm warranted
my warranty
(I think).
Dreams deferred,
justice denied,
nightmares shipped
with same day delivery,
and any deferral is denial,
so let me see the manager!

Oh wait.

I work here too
and am late for a double shift.
Broom in hand,
tap tap tapping
keys on register
registering that nothing unlocks
except time.
All that time.
Going to bank
from my soul
to account.

I want to see the manager!

But I live here,
in this place,
and I make it again, again
but do not benefit.

Why must janitors
tread so quietly
on floors they maintain?

Anxiety

Anxiety is
flammable concrete
the type that encases lungs,
weighs down
but burns
and agitates like that collapsing building you saw
on that car ride long ago,

when mother, angry at father but driving you all,

screamed and yelled
and you wished more than anything else to escape

into that ever-expanding horizon.
You knew then
that you would be running
and going nowhere
for miles and miles, even now.

Death of America

Are we living
during the death
of American freedom?
Probably not.
It's died before
so often
that I'm not sure
it ever lived.
Still birth
on sterile table
Dr. Frankenstein yelling…
nothing.
Fuck.
We missed freedom, y'all.
It was around for about a week in 2008.
Barely too.
So, we drown in barley fields.
Drowning face down
in shallow reflecting pools.

Untitled

Life is a dictionary,
full of meaning,
but its pages
are curiously blank.
I wonder,
am I supposed to ink stain
those stapled dead trees?
Collectively, I am told "yes,"
by a great exhaling
of digital,

o   n   l   i   n   e

confusion.

Untitled

The cars break down too often on that stretch of space. You know the spot, where 38th goes from city street to interstate and you have second to decide— Chicago or Lafayette Road? The latter spits you out on the far northwest corner of Indy-town with its concrete plains, once Midwest fields, then shopping malls, then abandoned post-industrial space, and now grass creeps back through the cracks. And on days when climate permits city folk roll into makeshift markets for day-by-day sales. They sell all manner of things— shirts and shoes and flags and cheap electronics.

The blue plastic tents whiz by my window as I drive into that area for the third time this week.

And I see those broken-down cars.

Cracked windshields, duct tape on outer hull as standard fix.

I see those cars try to reach the speed needed for the brief stretch of road and fail. Their engines' heart finally giving way to congestion. How many miles did they go before this fate? The car's owner sits in shade along the berm. This is the fare to fly these concrete corridors, here in a forgotten— rediscovered— Midwest place.

Hugs Not Drugs

Old smokers ask
       if
               I have a smoke to spare
and I have to report,

                                       sadly,
               that 1990s propaganda
worked
and that I can only offer
                                   hugs, not drugs.

Twentieth century laments.

Untitled

When the fires come
and waters rise
they will not
be a force of justice.
No. Nothing so anthropomorphic.
It's foolish,
attributing disaster to
karma's blade,
dontcha know?
Instead, those who perish
will be random,
and also, by design.
Those already forced to slums.
Those without privileges.
Unlike fire's rage,
and water's torrent,
our societies are
anthropocentric, and
our greed
and bias
reflect back
in horrifying,
staggering,
death toll statistics.
When the great dying
reaches such a place
that this place is
no longer tenable
for the long haul.
Profit margins
(calculated down to the
smallest
margin of errors)
the rich will do
what they think they are due

and dutifully climb high,
(oh, so high)
in dick-shaped rockets
blasting off,
fucking us all,
as they sail
to the stars to fuck further
some future we are not.
No worries, though.
They will wave
and pose
for selfies!
POST!
Onto facebooks
those photos go
so our faces can behold
how to smile, and thrive,
in this Anthropocene.

Dam Hysteria

The world gathered in panic. In streets, and marketplaces, in town squares, and schoolhouse buildings. The world crowded onto the digital stage and began speaking faster and faster. Do NOT Panic! the moderators sang. They modulated in modes that we could not understand. Panic swept through us like wildfire. The brush had grown too thick for us to think. No, poet! Someone yelled. We are thinking clearly. Don't tell us this is hysteria. This is panic. We see what is coming. We live on the streets, in the world, and we can read graffiti. We know the writing on the wall. Colleges elected; assassinations rang out like church bells. Is it a wedding or funeral? The bride and groom appeared, clasping each other in a casket and we smelled the truth. It was both. We were married in death. And not even death could do us apart. The digital stage shrank like melting ice caps as one by one doors slammed shut. They shuttered the modern café culture, and we were pushed out further and further until panic became a religion. A holy gospel. The moderators told us to be calm. They pleaded with us to REMAIN calm. But the ocean was moving, freed from ice, and the waves grew taller and taller. On the horizon we saw the men who know, or think they know, how to sail such historical hysterical waves. We swelled. We chased. We would sink these men who had caused so much pain. Into a dam we went, damnation for the nation and all who followed. Our hysteria and panic, the only thing we had to eat like bread to begging lips, was the only thing, the only sane thing, we could cling to. Into the dam our waves crashed. Our energy became the energy for a man atop the dam who pulled the levers and let us out with fixed regularity. He hoped to power his fortunes of design. The dam creaked and on the face of the operating dam man I saw… panic. Hysteria perhaps?

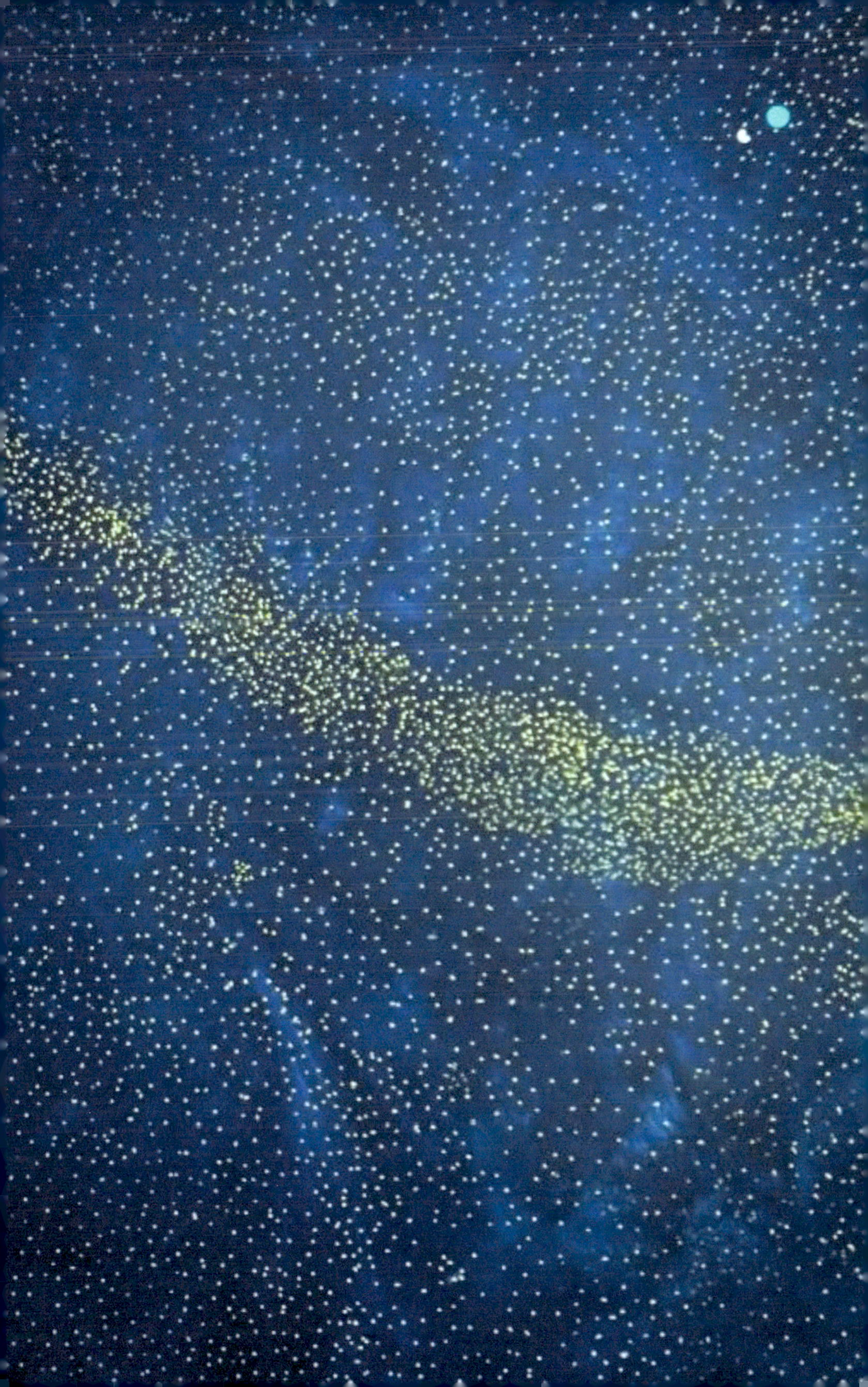

Acknowledgements and a Note on Publishing

I wrote the first poem that led to this book in the summer of 2014. The following fall I began my doctoral studies at Purdue University. Over the next four years I would write the majority of these poems in *Vienna Café*. For those of you not familiar with West Lafayette, Indiana, *Vienna* is hands-down the best place in the state to get a cup of coffee, good food, and enjoy a long conversation.

When I read this collection now, I think of the friends and comrades I had there, of the smell of strong coffee, and the oscillating emotions of fear and hope that constituted 2014-2018. In that time, I saw the final years of the Obama administration, the rise of Trump, and the worsening crisis of neo-Nazis, KKK members, and the so-called "alt-right" establish itself from margin to center.

Online spaces, too, took on ever stranger and deeper connotations as we wrestled with this thing that had been created, which had seeped into our daily lives, and was not noticeable until looked at in hindsight.

But there were more than just signs of hope. In that same café friends and I held meetings and actions, and planned protests and sit-ins. We held open poetry mics to celebrate art and community, and further bring people together in organizing. The resistance to injustice was, and is, strong. I continue to find my hope there.

For the next four years after that, I lived in Indianapolis and edited this collection, occasionally adding some pieces, during the height of the COVID lockdown, the George Floyd Protests, and the January 6th insurrection attempt.

It felt like a time apt for apocalyptic writing. Like a modern-day Apostle Paul penning letters about end-times, community ideals, and how to find salvation. Yet through all of that we continued to create countless traces of ourselves with each day spent in the digital sphere. The things we liked, or shared, or rage posted about, or emailed, or tweeted, or recorded were testaments to continuing to live. We are a literature, I found, in a vast sea of electronic connectivity.

But what will happen to our digital selves when we, and our time, are gone? Will it be possible to be hopeful as others scroll through our dystopias, utopias, and online enclaves? These poems attempt to at least explore some answers.

I have many people to thank for this book, too many to thank, but those who deserve special recognition are Ricardo Quintana-Vallejo and Carmine Di Biase. Both read the manuscript for this book in different stages and offered huge help in shaping and polishing it into a coherent collection. I am also indebted to my friends and colleagues Guillermo Caballero and Michelle Campbell who helped co-organize the "People's Mic" at *Vienna* while we were at Purdue University.

I performed many of these poems for the first time at those open mics. The audience feedback was invaluable.

Finally, I want to thank my friend and partner Allison. To her this book, like everything, I dedicate.

I am also excited to announce that this book is part of a new project at North Meridian Review— North Meridian Books. At Purdue, and then later when I began teaching in Indianapolis, a group of us began discussing launching a journal. We did this in 2019, and during those early conversations Ricardo and I mulled over creating an imprint for books that would work with authors of the journal to develop projects that found gatekeeping and market concerns unviable for their books.

The Digital Self was initially picked up by two different publishers, but due to a mixture of COVID and incompetence it was left languishing in a never-ending cycle of "wait" from editors. At that point, I re-opened the conversation with Ricardo, and others who had joined the journal, to launch the book arm of North Meridian. I know many snobs have choice words for the so-called "self-publishing" industry, but fortunately this book and this press is not for them. I often remind people that Donald Trump has found traditional publishers for his work, while Virginia Woolf launched a press to self-publish her books. If we at North Meridian fall somewhere between Trump and Woolf I will be very satisfied. At the end of the day isn't that all any of us can expect?

The Digital Self will be a first title in a series followed by many more. Already we have wonderful collections of poems, translations, novels, and academic studies joining the queue for NMB.

Dear reader, thank you for joining us in this venture. To the stars, from this old world, may we venture and find a place that is singular in its complexity and nuanced in its peace.

Wesley R. Bishop
Founding and Managing Editor
North Meridian Press
Calhoun County, Alabama

Made in the USA
Columbia, SC
28 November 2023